THE SEVEN HILLS
OF CHRISTMAS

THE SEVEN HILLS OF CHRISTMAS

POOJA LULLA

RUPA

Angels And Stars Of My Tree . . .
What Would Christmas Be Without Thee?

Contents

1

A Home Near The Hills

Sophie's family lived by a railroad. Their tiny house was right below a range of tall and snowy hills. There were seven hills in all, and they were called 'The Seven Hills of Christmas'.

Some people believed that strange and magical creatures lived on the hills. Some even said that Father Christmas lived on the last hill, at the very top.

But no one knew if it was true. For no one had been able to climb up the hills or make the journey to the top.

Sophie often spent hours watching the hills, wondering if the stories were true. But except for a

few sparrows and squirrels, she never saw anyone come down.

Sophie's father looked after the railroad. In the winter, he shovelled the snow that fell on the tracks.

His job didn't fetch him too much money. And so, Sophie and her baby brother didn't have too many toys.

Sophie spent most of her time helping her mother with the household chores. When she would finish, she would run to the tracks and watch the trains go by.

CHOO! CHOO! The trains would come, whistling cheerfully.

CHUFF! CHUFF! They would puff steam out of their smokestacks.

DING! DING! Their bells would ring making merry little sounds.

CHUG! CHUG! They would rattle along the tracks.

The trains' wagons were always full of smiling children. Some of them would wave to Sophie. Sophie would always wave back. The children would tell her that they were going to visit the most beautiful places of the world.

Sophie's eyes would light up.

'How I wish,' she would often look at the hills and say, 'that I too could ride on a train. How I wish I too could see the most beautiful places of the world! Nothing would make me happier!'

After the trains would go by, Sophie would pick up the bits of coal that had fallen off. Coal was very expensive and her family could hardly afford any. She would carefully put the small black lumps into her pockets and take them home to her mother. Sophie's mother was always happy to see the coal. The wind that blew down the hills made her feel very cold and the coal was always useful to make a warm fire.

2

The Morning Of Christmas Eve

When the morning of Christmas Eve came, Sophie woke up very early. She looked out of the window and saw that the world outside had turned white. It had snowed the previous night. Her father was on the tracks, clearing the snow.

Sophie ate her breakfast quickly and went to help her mother. She was looking forward to the day's chore. Her father had brought a small fir tree home and her mother wanted her to help decorate it for Christmas. Sophie painted a few pinecones and strung some popcorn to hang around the tree.

When she finished, she put her coat on and ran to the tracks. It was time for the train to go by.

'My shovel's broken,' Sophie's father told her when she reached the tracks. 'If it snows again, I'll have to the clear the tracks with my hands.'

Sophie hoped that it wouldn't snow anymore. Snow could make hands burn and fingers freeze. She didn't want her father to pick it up with his hands. She sat with her father and waited for the train, while he tried to fix his shovel.

CHOO! CHOO! The train soon came whistling and tooting cheerily.

CHUFF! CHUFF! It blew wisps of silvery steam in to the cold morning air.

DING! DING! Its bells clanged, sounding even livelier today.

CHUG! CHUG! It rambled merrily on the tracks.

As always, the train was full of some joyful-looking children.

'We are going away for Christmas,' a boy told Sophie. 'We are going to see some of the most beautiful places in the world! China! France! Italy! Russia! India! And many more!'

'How lucky you are!' Sophie said, waving back. 'I have only read about these places in books. Have a good journey and a wonderful Christmas!'

The train soon disappeared into a tunnel near the hills. Sophie found a few pieces of coal. She picked them up and put them into her coat pocket.

'I'll give them to Mother for Christmas!'

She then looked at the seven hills and sighed, 'How I wish I too could ride on a train! How I wish I too could see the beautiful places of the world! Nothing would make me happier!'

Later that morning, there was a very heavy snowfall. Thousands of snowflakes fell from a purple-blue sky. The windows of Sophie's house turned frosty and the roof white.

An icy wind blew with all its might. It rattled the doors and windows of the little house so hard that Sophie's baby brother got a fright.

'Waa-aah!' the baby wailed, making his little cheeks quite red.

'Atishoo! Atishoo!' Sophie's mother sneezed and shivered.

Sophie's father looked troubled. A whole lot of snow was falling on the tracks. Sophie knew that he hadn't been able to his fix his shovel and was worried about clearing the snow with his hands.

'I wish my family wasn't so unhappy right before Christmas Day,' Sophie thought.

She then looked up at the hills and sighed, 'How I wish that the baby had a toy to cheer him up! And Mother had a warm shawl! A new shovel would make Father so happy! If only my family got all these for Christmas, it wouldn't matter if I never got to ride on a train.'

3

The Sack On The Tracks

Sophie was clearing the table after lunch, when she heard a sound outside the window. She peered through the frosty glass, but could hardly see what was outside.

'I hope more snow hasn't fallen on the tracks,' she prayed.

She wore her boots and tied a scarf around her head. She buttoned up her coat and went out of the house.

It was still snowing outside. A chilly wind was blowing down the hills.

Sophie ran to the tracks. An enormous sack was lying there. She carefully undid the string and looked inside. Her eyes grew wide.

The sack was full of some charming toys!

Smart tin soldiers, elegant rocking horses, teddy bears with sailor caps and blue bows, pretty dolls in long dresses made of frill, shiny silver rattles, animals carved out of wood, toy ships with sails, model trains, brightly painted blocks, doll's tea sets, tiny carousels, drum sets, monkeys made of socks, and even a tinkling music box!

Sophie rubbed her eyes. She had never seen so many toys together before.

What beautiful toys!' she said. 'I wonder where this sack came from! And I wonder whom the toys belong to!'

'I know where the sack came from,' a squirrel chattered, rolling a nut out of a tree. 'I saw it fall down the hills.'

'The Seven Hills of Christmas?' Sophie asked, surprised. 'That means the sack must belong to Father Christmas! Who else would have a sackful of toys right before Christmas Day?'

She stood up and lifted the sack with all her might.

'I must take these toys back to Father Christmas at once,' Sophie said. 'Or else, the children they are meant for will be very disappointed when they wake up and don't see any presents on Christmas Day'

'But no one has climbed the hills before,' the squirrel told Sophie. 'And no one knows if Father Christmas really lives on them.'

'I will try,' Sophie said. 'I will climb the hills and look for him. And I will try my best.'

She said 'goodbye' to the squirrel and began walking towards the seven hills, carrying the enormous sack on her little back.

4

The First Hill of Christmas

Sophie walked for a very long while before she reached the foot of the first hill.

The sunshine was gentle here and the sky was marble-blue.

A cool breeze ruffled Sophie's hair. The trees had barks of silver and the rocks and shrubs had a sprinkling of snow. The air felt light and had the fragrance of cherries.

Sophie started to climb up the hill when she heard a strange voice.

'Who dares go up my hill?' the voice asked.

Sophie saw a fox jump out from under some rocks. It had a furry coat that was as red as fire, small slanting eyes, and a tail that was thick and bushy.

'Who are you?' Sophie asked the fox.

'I am the Keeper of the First Hill of Christmas,' the fox replied. 'Where are you going with those toys?'

'I found them on the tracks,' Sophie answered, 'I am taking them to Father Christmas.'

The fox laughed. 'What a silly girl you are! I have often seen you near the railroad. And I know that you don't have too many toys. Why don't you keep these toys for yourself? You can even give some to your baby brother.'

'Oh no!' Sophie said, shaking her head. 'These toys belong to Father Christmas. I will return them to him.'

'Then how about keeping just one or two?' the fox suggested with a sly grin. 'No one is watching. No one will know I promise I won't tell a soul'

'No, thank you,' Sophie said. 'I would never do that. Not even if I knew no one was watching. Or even if you promised not to tell anyone.'

The fox smiled at Sophie. 'I haven't met a girl like you ever before. I will be happy if you climb up my hill.'

Sophie thanked the fox and climbed up the First Hill of Christmas.

5

The Second Hill Of Christmas

After sometime, Sophie reached the foot of the second hill.

The wind was very strong here. The trees were leafless and bare. The sun was shining very brightly in a yellow-blue sky, making the snow shimmer just like a mirror. Dry leaves rustled around Sophie's feet and there was a dash of ginger in the air.

Sophie was about to go further when a strange voice called out to her.

'Who dares go up my hill? Who? Who?'

Sophie saw an owl sitting on the branch of a tree.

It had big yellow eyes that it was shielding with its speckled wings.

'Who are you?' She asked the owl.

'I am the Keeper of the Second Hill of Christmas,' the owl yawned and rubbed its eyes. 'I cannot sleep. The wind has blown away all the leaves. My tree has turned bare. There isn't a single shady spot left to shelter me from the sun's glare.'

Sophie wondered how she could shelter the old owl from the sun's glare. She then remembered the scarf she had around her head. She knew she would feel cold if she took it out, but she felt sorry for the owl.

Quietly, Sophie put the sack down and took her scarf out. The wind howled. It tangled Sophie's hair and almost blew the scarf away. Sophie held on to it tightly and carefully tied its corners to the branches of the tree.

'I have made you a tent,' she then told the owl. 'Its shade will shelter you from the sun's glare. Do try and sleep now.'

The owl yawned. It drooped its eyes. 'Do go up my hill,' it mumbled and fell fast asleep.

'Thank you and sweet dreams,' Sophie whispered to the sleeping owl and then tiptoed up the Second Hill of Christmas.

6

The Third Hill Of Christmas

In a little while, Sophie reached the foot of the third hill.

The sky here was a smoky grey. A drizzly rain was falling all over. The trees were dripping wet. There was no breeze and the wind was very still. The snow had turned into slush. The air felt damp and had a trace of cinnamon.

'It must have been raining here,' Sophie thought, as she trudged along the slushy snow.

Once again, she heard a strange voice.

'Who dares go up my hill?' the voice growled.

Sophie saw a leopard leap out from behind a tree. It had a long sturdy tail and a coat of light-yellow fur. Its eyes were misty and green and shone like a cat's. There were many spots on the leopard's back.

Some were white, some were grey and some were black.

'Who are you?' Sophie asked the leopard.

'I am the Keeper of the Third Hill of Christmas,' the leopard said and sighed. 'As you can see, there was rainfall on my hill. The rainwater has made some of my spots fade. Some of them have turned grey and light. Some have even turned white. I am no longer the beautiful leopard I used to be.'

Sophie put the sack down and pulled out one of the coal pieces from her pocket. She had hoped to give it to her mother as a Christmas present, but she knew that she had to help the leopard now.

She climbed onto the leopard's back and said, 'Please be very still,'

She then darkened the faded spots with the coal. In a short while, all the spots on the leopard's back were once again black.

The leopard looked at them happily.

'Thank you, little girl,' it told Sophie gratefully, 'please go up my hill.'

Sophie thanked the leopard. She got off its back, picked up the sack, and made her way up the Third Hill of Christmas.

7

The Fourth Hill Of Christmas

Soon, Sophie reached the foot of the fourth hill.

It was much colder here. The wind was stiff and the sunshine pale. The sky was a smeary blue. A deep carpet of snow had formed on the ground. The scent of crushed vanilla pods filled the air.

Sophie walked very slowly, so that her boots wouldn't get caught in the snow.

Here too, she heard a strange voice. It was quite small this time.

Who dares go up my hill?'

Sophie saw a young rabbit sitting on a log. Its fur was as white as the hill's snow. Its tail looked like a cotton-ball, and its nose and eyes like buttons.

'Who are you?' Sophie kneeled and asked the rabbit.

'I am the Keeper of the Fourth Hill of Christmas,' the rabbit said in a whisper-like voice.

'I know that I am a rabbit,' the rabbit sighed, 'but I have never seen anyone like me before. I don't even know what I look like.'

'How terrible it must be not to know what one looks like?' Sophie thought.

Quietly, she put the sack down and picked up some snow. Her hands stung. The snow was freezing cold. She began patting it into a snowball. Her fingers ached and turned blue. But she didn't stop and went on smoothening the snow, till it took the shape of a rabbit.

She then pulled out the buttons of her coat and used them as the snow-rabbit's eyes and nose.

'This is what you and most other rabbits look like.'

The rabbit looked on. Wonder filled both its eyes.

It clapped its tiny paws.

'How clever!' it squealed happily. 'Now I know what I look like! Please do go up my hill!'

Sophie thanked the rabbit and crossed the Fourth Hill of Christmas.

8

The Fifth Hill Of Christmas

It was evening by the time Sophie reached the foot of the fifth hill.

The air here was thick and had the hint of caramel. A thin coat of ice had covered all the shrubs and trees of this hill. The ground felt slippery and was coated with ice. An icy wind raged and hail fell from a steel-grey sky.

Sophie felt very, very cold. Her breath turned to frosty wisps and she had to keep shielding her eyes.

She held on to the sack tightly and walked on very slowly, taking care not to slip.

As on the other hills, there was a voice here too.

'Who dares go up my hill?' the voice grunted.

Sophie saw a bear come out of a cave. It had brown fur that had turned scruffy and was covered with icicles.

Who are you?' Sophie asked the bear.

'I am the Keeper of the Fifth Hill of Christmas,' the bear said in a hoarse voice.

'The water on my hill has frozen and turned into ice. My throat is parched and my mouth is dry. I haven't had a sip of water to drink in days. I am very, very thirsty.'

The sun was beginning to set and Sophie had hoped to reach the top of the hill before nightfall. She knew that she would be late if she stopped to help the bear. Still, she put the sack down.

She took the coal left in her pocket and kept it on the ice. She then picked up two stones and rubbed them together.

Nothing happened. Sophie tried again. And again. And after what must have been a few dozen tries, a tiny spark appeared between the two stones.

Quickly, Sophie used the spark to light the coal. It began to burn. The ice around it melted slowly and formed a small pool of water.

'Here's some water for you to drink,' Sophie told the bear.

The bear thirstily lapped up all the water.

It then turned to Sophie and bowed its head. 'I'll be happy, little girl, if you go up my hill.'

Sophie thanked the bear and hurried up the Fifth Hill of Christmas.

9

The Sixth Hill Of Christmas

It had grown quite dark by the time Sophie reached the foot of the sixth hill.

It was colder than ever here. The wind was icy and bit into Sophie's cheeks. Her lips chapped and her teeth chattered. Her feet burned, for the soles of her boots had thinned. The air felt heavy and had a tinge of freshly-ground almonds.

Sophie looked around and saw that there were no shrubs or trees on this hill. There was nothing here for miles - not even rocks. Only chunks of plain white ice covered this hill.

But the sky looked beautiful from here. It was dark and velvety and had thousands of sparkling stars.

Once again, Sophie started to climb the hill when she heard a strange voice.

'Who dares go up my hill?' the voice roared.

Sophie saw a lion stride out of a shadow. It had a beautiful flowing mane and was holding a young goat beneath its strong forelimbs.

'Who are you?' Sophie asked the lion, trying not to be afraid.

'I am the Keeper of the Sixth Hill of Christmas,' the lion roared.

'I found this goat wandering on my hill. I am going to keep it here forever. My hill is plain and bare. The goat will make a pretty sight for me to look at, before I sleep every night.'

'Please, mighty lion!' the goat begged. 'Please, let me go! I promised my family that I would be home for Christmas.'

Sophie hoped that the lion would let the goat go. Like the goat, she too wanted to be at home with her family on Christmas Day. But she understood how the lion felt. Its hill was empty and bare, and she knew how badly it must want something pretty to look at.

'Please, let the goat go,' Sophie told the lion bravely. 'Everyone should be at home with their families on Christmas Day'

The lion thought for a while and then said, 'All right, I will let this goat go. But only if you find me another one. One that is prettier than this goat. One that I can look at every night.'

Sophie pointed to the sky.

'Look at the sky! There's a goat there!'

The lion looked up and saw that some of the stars had gathered together in the shape of a goat.

'Isn't that twinkling goat a far prettier sight than this poor weeping goat?' Sophie said.

'You are right,' the lion said, putting the goat down. 'I will let this goat go and look at the one in the sky every night. I will also let you climb up my hill.'

The goat scurried away and Sophie thanked the lion.

She then picked up the sack and climbed up the Sixth Hill of Christmas.

10

The Seventh Hill Of Christmas

After what seemed a very long time, Sophie reached the foot of the seventh hill.

The sky above was a rich blue. It looked like a sheet of smooth silk. The moon shone on it brightly, looking like a silver mirror. The stars were twinkling brightly and felt close enough to touch. The wind felt wonderfully warm, even though snowflakes were twirling to the ground. The air was crisp and had the scent of nutmeg.

'What a beautiful hill!' Sophie thought. 'But I won't stop to admire it now. I must find Father Christmas first. It's already very late.'

No one stopped Sophie here. And so, she walked on as fast as she could.

Soon, Sophie reached the top of the hill. A light was shining in the distance. It seemed to be coming from a cluster of fir trees. Sophie's legs were trembling with tiredness and she felt out of breath. Yet, she followed the light and walked on.

After a short while, she reached a small house that was hidden behind the trees. A patch of snow had covered its roof. Sparkling flecks of red were rising from the chimney.

'I hope whoever lives here knows where Father Christmas is,' Sophie thought as she rang the bell near the door.

A few minutes later, the door opened. Sophie looked up and gasped. Standing before her was a man holding a candlelight. Sophie saw that he had a long green coat and crinkly, twinkling eyes. His beard was flowing and white. She thought he looked kind and gentle and old enough to be her or anyone else's grandfather.

'Who - who are you?' Sophie asked, her heart beating very fast.

'I am the Keeper of The Seventh Hill of Christmas,' the man said in a soft, kind voice. 'Some people call me

Father Christmas.' Who are you, little girl? And what are you doing on my hill?'

'I — I am Sophie,' Sophie heard herself say. 'I live near the railroad below the hills. I found these toys on the tracks. I think they are yours and I've come here to return them to you. I hope you will be able to take them to the children you have made them for, before Christmas Day'

'Why, yes! Those are my toys,' Father Christmas said, looking quite surprised. 'The wind was very strong here today. It must have blown the sack away'

Father Christmas then took the sack from Sophie. He took it to a long wooden table outside his house and turned it over. The toys tumbled out.

Father Christmas began counting them. He then looked at Sophie like she was very strange.

'There isn't a single toy missing from the sack. Does that mean you haven't taken even one for yourself?'

'I haven't, Father Christmas,' Sophie said truthfully. 'Not a single one.'

'Hmm,' Father Christmas said. 'No one has returned lost toys before. And no one has been allowed to climb up the hills. You must be a very special girl. The Keepers of The Seven Hills of Christmas would have never let you come up otherwise.'

'She is, Father Christmas,' some voices said.

Sophie saw the creatures she had met on the way — the fox, the owl, the leopard, the rabbit, the bear and the lion — walking towards the house.

11

The Keepers' Feast

'I have never met anyone as honest,' the fox told Father Christmas. 'She didn't want to keep the toys for herself. Not even a single one!'

'I haven't met anyone as generous,' the owl said. 'She gave me her scarf, even though it was windy and cold.'

'I think she's kind,' the leopard said. 'She darkened my spots with the coal she was saving for her mother!'

'Caring too,' the rabbit said. 'She made a rabbit out of the icy snow and even used her coat buttons, just so that I know what I look like.'

'Patient,' the bear said. 'She stopped to make me a drink of water, even though she was running late.'

'Brave and wise'; the lion said. 'She stopped me from doing something very selfish tonight.'

'Do reward her, Father Christmas,' the creatures said together.

'Sophie is, indeed, an extraordinary little girl,' Father Christmas said.

'She left her safe dry home and came, all the way, here to return the toys. Just so that the children they are meant for don't wake up disappointed on Christmas Day. Come, let's first ask her to join our feast. She must be very hungry.'

Father Christmas was right. Climbing up The Seven Hills of Christmas had made Sophie very, very hungry.

Shyly, she sat with him and the others at the wooden table.

All the Keepers had brought something to the feast that they wanted to share with Sophie.

The fox had brought a jar of cherries from the first hill. The cherries had been soaked in a thick syrup of sugar and were delightfully sour and sweet.

The owl, who was now wide awake, had brought a tin of gingerbread from the second hill. The gingerbread was crisp and fragrant and scrumptious with every bite.

The leopard had brought a box of warm biscuits from the third hill. They had a generous sprinkling of cinnamon which, Sophie thought, tasted very nice.

The rabbit had carried a pouch of soft vanilla-flavoured marshmallows, all the way up, from the fourth hill. They looked like tiny snowballs and Sophie thought that they were the softest marshmallows in the world.

The bear had brought a pan of chewy-brown caramel from the fifth hill. The caramel was sticky and sweet and a whole lot of fun to eat.

The lion had brought a bag of marzipan fruits from the sixth hill.

The marzipan had been made with finely ground almonds and sugar. Sophie thought that they were the most delicious fruits she had ever eaten.

When everyone had almost finished eating, Father Christmas brought a kettle of warm milk from his kitchen. He poured the milk into some mugs and garnished it with shavings of nutmeg. The nutmeg made the milk taste wonderful and Sophie feel warm and refreshed.

'I have never had such a wonderful feast before,' Sophie told her new friends. 'Thank you for asking me to join you.'

12

A Wish Comes True

When the feast was over, Father Christmas said, 'Sophie, will you come with me? We will go all over the world and give away the toys you found.'

Sophie rubbed her eyes. No other little girl or boy she knew had ever been asked something like this. Not even in their fanciest dreams!

'Yes, Father Christmas,' she said. 'I will.'

Father Christmas then took Sophie to the end of the Seventh Hill of Christmas.

The most beautiful train Sophie had ever seen stood there. It had a shiny red engine, a silver smokestack and three glossy wooden wagons.

A bright shining headlamp, that looked exactly like the moon in the sky, was in the front of the engine. Twinkling little stars hung on both its sides, looking just like fairy lights.

CHOO CHOO! The train whistled cheerily.

CHUFF! CHUFF! It smartly blew silvery-white clouds in to the cool night air.

DING! DING! Its bells jingled, making a magical sound.

Sophie gasped. 'I can't believe that I am going to ride with you, Father Christmas! And give away Christmas presents! On a train!'

'This is no ordinary train, Sophie,' Father Christmas said with a smile. 'This is The Christmas Train. It runs only once a year. On Christmas Eve. And, it goes all over the world in a single night!'

'But what will The Christmas Train ride on?' Sophie asked. 'I didn't see any tracks on the hills.'

'The Christmas Train doesn't ride on the hills,' Father Christmas replied. 'It rides in the sky. On special tracks. Look! Here they come now!'

WHOOSH! A gentle wind blew around the hill. And something very strange and very magical happened.

The wind whisked the clouds near the hill. And they slowly took the shape of train tracks.

'How wonderful!' Sophie said joyfully. 'I have never seen tracks made of clouds before!'

'These tracks appear only when I'm ready to leave on Christmas Eve,' Father Christmas said, shovelling some snow off the train with a sturdy-looking shovel. And they only last till Christmas morning.'

If you look at the sky at sunrise tomorrow, you will see them fading in the sunlight.'

Father Christmas put the toys into the wagons. 'Come aboard, Sophie,' he called.

Sophie sat in the train. She waved to the fox, the owl, the leopard, the rabbit, the bear and the lion and wondered if she would ever see them again.

CHUG! CHUG! CHUG! The Christmas Train hummed and smoothly glided onto the cloud-tracks.

The Christmas Train then took Father Christmas and Sophie all over the world.

To China! France! Italy! Russia! And India!

It halted above houses and Sophie watched as Father Christmas sent the toys she had found into windows and chimneys.

They went to all the other countries Sophie had only read of in books, or heard of from the children she had seen on the trains.

After they had gone all over the world, Father Christmas took a very sleepy Sophie home.

13

Christmas Morning

'What a lovely dream!' Sophie thought when she woke up the next morning. 'The sack of toys! The Seven Hills of Christmas! The enchanted creatures who were its Keepers! Father Christmas! The wonderful feast! And The Christmas Train that went all over the world on tracks made of clouds! It felt so real!'

Suddenly, she heard peals of laughter. She had never heard her family sound so happy before. She ran out of her room and saw her family sitting by the Christmas tree.

Her mother had a beautiful shawl draped around her shoulders. It was made of blue silk, and had stars and a moon embroidered on it with silver thread.

'Father Christmas brought me a shawl!' Sophie's mother said and laughed. 'It's making me feel so warm!'

'The shawl looks just like the sky of the Seventh Hill of Christmas that I saw in my dream!' Sophie thought.

'Look at the shovel Father Christmas brought me!' Sophie's father said merrily, showing Sophie a shovel that looked exacdy like the one Father Christmas had, on The Christmas Train. 'I'll be able to clear any amount of snow with it!'

'Ga Ga! Gee Gee!' Sophie's baby brother gurgled, like he wanted to say, 'Look at what Father Christmas brought me!'

A box of carved wooden animals was in the baby's hands. In it were a fox, an owl, a leopard, a rabbit, a bear and a lion! They looked exactly like the creatures Sophie had met on the hills!

'Does this mean that my other wish came true too?' Sophie wondered. 'Does this mean that I really climbed up the hills? Did I really meet all those enchanted creatures? And did I really go all over the world with Father Christmas on The Christmas Train?'

She ran to the window and looked out.

The sun was rising behind the hills.

And in the sky were some clouds shaped like tracks. They were fading away in the sunlight.

www.ingramcontent.com/pod-product-compliance
Lightning Source LLC
Chambersburg PA
CBHW051515260626

47162CB00008B/2982